W9-COZ-538

THE COMPLETE STORIES OF J.G. BALLARD

Works by J.G. Ballard

THE COMPLETE STORIES OF J.G. BALLARD

W. W. Norton & Company
New York · London

For information about permission to reproduce selections from this book, write to Permissions, W. W. Norton & Company, Inc., 500 Fifth Avenue, New York, NY 10110

For information about special discounts for bulk purchases, please contact W. W. Norton Special Sales at specialsales@wwnorton.com or 800-233-4830

Manufacturing by RR Donnelley, Harrisonburg, VA

Ballard, J. G., 1930–2009.
[Short stories]
The complete stories of J.G. Ballard. — 1st American ed.
p. cm.
Previously published as: The complete short stories.
Includes bibliographical references and index.
ISBN 978-0-393-07262-4
I. Title.
PR6052.A46A6 2009
823'.914—dc22
          2009018456

W. W. Norton & Company, Inc.
500 Fifth Avenue, New York, N.Y. 10110
www.wwnorton.com

W. W. Norton & Company Ltd.
Castle House, 75/76 Wells Street, London W1T 3QT

1 2 3 4 5 6 7 8 9 0

Contents

NEW STORIES FOR THE AMERICAN EDITION

INTRODUCTION

Martin Amis

I first came across Jim Ballard when I was a teenager in the 1960s. My father, Kingsley Amis, championed his work, calling him 'the brightest star in British postwar SF' (all purists call science fiction SF, and have the greatest contempt for 'sci fi'); and Jim was a frequent visitor to the house. He was, I thought, a charismatically handsome man, with a rich, resonant face and hot, busy eyes; and he talked in the cadences of extreme sarcasm, using abnormally heavy stresses (he wasn't being sarcastic; he was being gleefully emphatic). In retrospect I see that the friendship between the two did not survive Jim's increasing interest in experimentalism, which Kingsley always anathematised as 'buggering about with the reader'. But I always felt a strong surge of warmth whenever I saw Jim later on; funnily enough, he was an exceptionally lovable man, despite the ferocity of his imagination.

His imagination was formed by his wartime experience in Shanghai, where he was interned by the Japanese. He was thirteen, and took to camp life as he would to 'a huge slum family'. But it wasn't just the camp that formed him – it was the startlingly low value attached to human life, something he witnessed throughout his childhood. He once saw a rickshaw coolie being beaten to death ten feet from where he stood, and each morning as he was driven to school in an American limousine he saw 'a dead body every two hundred yards'. Then came the Japanese (and the feral antagonism that would give rise, most notably, to the rape of Nanking). 'People brought up in the social democracies of Western Europe,' he once told me, during a day-long interview in 1984, 'have no idea of this kind of savagery. No they don't, actually, and it's a good thing that they don't.'

It is interesting that his two most famous novels were both filmed by famous (and interesting) directors: *Empire of the Sun* by Steven Spielberg (an essentially optimistic artist who is nonetheless drawn to dark historical themes) and *Crash* by David Cronenberg (a much darker artist himself, and one who specialises in filming unfilmably rebarbative novels). *Empire*, as Ballard always called it, is the novel about Shanghai; *Crash* is animated by an obsession with the sexuality of the road accident – and is much the more typical. One is reminded that 'obsession' derives from the Latin *obsidere*, which means 'to lay siege to'. Ballard was beleaguered by obsession. In his work, mood and landscape are indivisible. He had very little curiosity about human beings in the conventional sense, i. e., as individuals (and a revealingly weak ear for dialogue); he was utterly visual, and his mind, like his settings, was in his own phrase 'lunar and abstract'.

Waywardly but intelligibly, *Empire of the Sun* – his greatest success – came as a kind of backhander to Ballard's most faithful admirers. The novel, which is utterly and unwontedly realistic, seemed a kind of betrayal of the Ballard mystique. The cultists felt that *Empire* showed how the author's imagination had been warped into such an outlandish shape; it was a naturalistic explanation of how he got that way. For the cultists (again, not very logically), it was as if the witchdoctor had drily revealed the secret of his charms.

Ballard began as a hardcore SF writer (his early stuff was published in such magazines as *Amazing Stories*, *Science Fantasy*, *New Worlds*, and the like). But the genre couldn't hold him. There followed four novels of poeticised apocalypse – *The Wind from Nowhere* (1961), *The Drowned World* (1962), *The Drought* (1964), and *The Crystal World* (1966) – where, with great relish, the planet is destroyed, respectively, by mega-hurricane, by flood, by heat, and by mineralisation. Then came his brutalist period, beginning in 1970 with *The Atrocity Exhibition*. Two chapter headings from that book will give you a fair intimation of the new emphasis: 'The Facelift of Princess Margaret' and 'Why I Want to Fuck Ronald Reagan'.

Brutalism elided into what might be called the years of mortar and steel, with *Crash* (1973), *Concrete Island* (1974), and *High-Rise* (1975), and then levelled out into a general preoccupation best evoked by another title – 'Myths of the Near Future'. The near future went on being his personal 'theme park' – a favourite phrase – until his death (despite a notable divagation into the past, with the beautiful and moving memoir *Miracles of Life*, published in 2008). The last novels, which include *Cocaine Nights* (1996) and *Super-Cannes* (2000), concerned themselves with the latent atavisms of corporate and ultra-privileged enclaves: the psychoses of the gated community.

Ballard brought to all these phases his kabbalistic skill in extrapolating from the present. This was his abiding question: what effect does the modern setting have on our psyches – the motion sculpture of the highways, the airport architecture, the culture of the shopping mall, the pervasiveness of pornography, and our dependence on ungrasped technologies? His tentative answer was perversity, which takes various forms, all of them (Ballard being Ballard) pathologically extreme. When he distanced himself from generic SF, he said that he was rejecting outer space in favour of 'inner space'. Inner space was always his beat.

As a man, Ballard was a great exemplar of the Flaubertian principle: writers should be orderly and predictable in their lives, so that they can be ferocious and sinister in their work. He lived in the dormitory precinct of Shepperton, in a semi-detached house which might as well have been called 'HisandHers' or 'Dunroamin', and there was the standard tomato-red Ford Escort in its slot in the little front garden. When I visited him in 1984, he said, 'All these French

Crash-freaks used to come out here to see me, expecting a miasma of child-molestation and drug abuse.' What they found was a robustly rounded and amazingly cheerful suburbanite.

I arrived at eleven in the morning, and his first words were 'Whisky! Gin! Vodka!' It was his only eccentricity of the day (and we both settled for coffee). In 1964 his wife Mary died, suddenly and dismayingly, on a family holiday, and Ballard at once resolved to raise the three children himself. To begin with he could only get through the day by drinking a large scotch every hour, starting at nine in the morning. It took him quite a while to push this back to six in the evening. I asked him, 'Was that difficult?' And he said, 'Difficult? It was like the Battle of Stalingrad.' But push it back he did, and everything suggests that he was a tolerant, pragmatic, and impeccably adoring father.

The last time I saw Jim, three or four years ago, was when my wife and I (and Will Self and his wife Deborah Orr) had dinner with him and his partner of forty years, Claire Walsh. He revealed in the restaurant that he had 'about two years to live. They tell me about two years.' This was said with instinctive courage, but with all the melancholy to be expected from a man who loved the miracle of life so ardently.

The short stories collected here span an entire creative life – all the way, from the first articulated words to the last. How to characterise them? Well, if H.H. Munro ('Saki') and Jorge Luis Borges had met, in Shanghai in 1930, and fallen in love, then J.G. Ballard would have been their child. He is an expert at the Saki-esque twist, the sting in the tail; and, like Borges, he addresses his fantastic figments with glazed and invincible conviction.

Ballard's evolution or trajectory, as described above, is detectable here in fragmentary form. In the early stories we see him pushing hard against the boundaries of conventional SF. In this genre, the most often-visited future is the dystopia of overpopulation. Watch what Ballard does with it:

> Noon talk on Millionth Street . . .
> 'Take a westbound express to 495th Avenue, cross over to a Redline elevator and go up a thousand levels to Plaza Terminal. Carry on south from there and you'll find it between 568th Avenue and 422nd Street.'

In his (later-disowned) first novel, *The Wind from Nowhere*, Ballard conjures a fast-moving and city-swallowing lateral avalanche of concrete and steel. In 'The Concentration City' we are shown a planetwide highrise – and a world without sea and without sky.

He never abandoned the science-fictional tour de force, as an option for certain global or cosmic ideas; but the focus soon moves toward the inner space of the mind. See 'Manhole 69', in which various volunteers are scientifically conditioned to do without sleep (the outcome is brilliantly terrifying); see 'The

Sudden Afternoon', in which a man finds that his memory – and then his entire identity – is being invaded by a murderer. These are literalistic versions of the broader tendency: the psychic distortions and intrusions that await us in the 'near-after'.

And Ballard's mind? It continually circles back to the experiences recounted in *Empire* (and in *Miracles of Life*). On the one hand, the drained swimming pools, the abandoned villas, and the wraithlike wanderers in a landscape from which all recognisable human activity has absented itself; and, on the other, the squalor, the hellish proximities, and the vigilant cruelty that derives from the camp. All these fables are written in a prose that veers from the higher-utilitarian to something ecstatic, melodious, and creamily precise: a style all his own.

J.G. Ballard will quite possibly be remembered as the most original English writer of the last century. It is a solecism to talk about degrees of uniqueness (either you are or you aren't), but Ballard was somehow uniquely unique. He used to like saying that writers were 'one-man teams' (and needed the 'support' of their readers). But he was also a one-man genre. He was impregnably *sui generis*. No one is or was remotely like him.

—London, May 2009

AUTHOR'S INTRODUCTION

Short stories are the loose change in the treasury of fiction, easily ignored beside the wealth of novels available, an over-valued currency that often turns out to be counterfeit. At its best, in Borges, Ray Bradbury and Edgar Allan Poe, the short story is coined from precious metal, a glint of gold that will glow for ever in the deep purse of your imagination.

Short stories have always been important to me. I like their snapshot quality, their ability to focus intensely on a single subject. They're also a useful way of trying out the ideas later developed at novel length. Almost all my novels were first hinted at in short stories, and readers of *The Crystal World*, *Crash* and *Empire of the Sun* will find their seeds germinating somewhere in this collection.

When I started writing, fifty years ago, short stories were immensely popular with readers, and some newspapers printed a new short story every day. Sadly, I think that people at present have lost the knack of reading short stories, a response perhaps to the baggy and long-winded narratives of television serials. Young writers, myself included, have always seen their first novels as a kind of virility test, but so many novels published today would have been better if they had been recast as short stories. Curiously, there are many perfect short stories, but no perfect novels.

The short story still survives, especially in science fiction, which makes the most of its closeness to the folk tale and the parable. Many of the stories in this collection were first published in science fiction magazines, though readers at the time loudly complained that they weren't science fiction at all.

But I was interested in the real future that I could see approaching, and less in the invented future that science fiction preferred. The future, needless to say, is a dangerous area to enter, heavily mined and with a tendency to turn and bite your ankles as you stride forward. A correspondent recently pointed out to me that the poetry-writing computers in *Vermilion Sands* are powered by valves. And why don't all those sleek people living in the future have PCs and pagers?

I could only reply that *Vermilion Sands* isn't set in the future at all, but in a kind of visionary present – a description that fits the stories in this book and almost everything else I have written. But oh for a steam-powered computer and a wind-driven television set. Now, there's an idea for a short story ...

J.G. Ballard, 2001

PRIMA BELLADONNA

I first met Jane Ciracylides during the Recess, that world slump of boredom, lethargy and high summer which carried us all so blissfully through ten unforgettable years, and I suppose that may have had a lot to do with what went on between us. Certainly I can't believe I could make myself as ridiculous now, but then again, it might have been just Jane herself.

Whatever else they said about her, everyone had to agree she was a beautiful girl, even if her genetic background was a little mixed. The gossips at Vermilion Sands soon decided there was a good deal of mutant in her, because she had a rich patina-golden skin and what looked like insects for eyes, but that didn't bother either myself or any of my friends, one or two of whom, like Tony Miles and Harry Devine, have never since been quite the same to their wives.

We spent most of our time in those days on the balcony of my apartment off Beach Drive, drinking beer – we always kept a useful supply stacked in the refrigerator of my music shop on the street level – yarning in a desultory way and playing i-Go, a sort of decelerated chess which was popular then. None of the others ever did any work; Harry was an architect and Tony Miles sometimes sold a few ceramics to the tourists, but I usually put a couple of hours in at the shop each morning, getting off the foreign orders and turning the beer.

One particularly hot lazy day I'd just finished wrapping up a delicate soprano mimosa wanted by the Hamburg Oratorio Society when Harry phoned down from the balcony.

'Parker's Choro-Flora?' he said. 'You're guilty of overproduction. Come up here. Tony and I have something beautiful to show you.'

When I went up I found them grinning happily like two dogs who had just discovered an interesting tree.

'Well?' I asked. 'Where is it?'

Tony tilted his head slightly. 'Over there.'

I looked up and down the street, and across the face of the apartment house opposite.

'Careful,' he warned me. 'Don't gape at her.'

I slid into one of the wicker chairs and craned my head round cautiously.

'Fourth floor,' Harry elaborated slowly, out of the side of his mouth. 'One left from the balcony opposite. Happy now?'

'Dreaming,' I told him, taking a long slow focus on her. 'I wonder what else she can do?'

Harry and Tony sighed thankfully. 'Well?' Tony asked.

'She's out of my league,' I said. 'But you two shouldn't have any trouble. Go over and tell her how much she needs you.'

Harry groaned. 'Don't you realize, this one is poetic, emergent, something straight out of the primal apocalyptic sea. She's probably divine.'

The woman was strolling around the lounge, rearranging the furniture, wearing almost nothing except a large metallic hat. Even in shadow the sinuous lines of her thighs and shoulders gleamed gold and burning. She was a walking galaxy of light. Vermilion Sands had never seen anything like her.

'The approach has got to be equivocal,' Harry continued, gazing into his beer. 'Shy, almost mystical. Nothing urgent or grabbing.'

The woman stooped down to unpack a suitcase and the metal vanes of her hat fluttered over her face. She saw us staring at her, looked around for a moment and lowered the blinds.

We sat back and looked thoughtfully at each other, like three triumvirs deciding how to divide an empire, not saying too much, and one eye watching for any chance of a double-deal.

Five minutes later the singing started.

At first I thought it was one of the azalea trios in trouble with an alkaline pH, but the frequencies were too high. They were almost out of the audible range, a thin tremolo quaver which came out of nowhere and rose up the back of the skull.

Harry and Tony frowned at me.

'Your livestock's unhappy about something,' Tony told me. 'Can you quieten it down?'

'It's not the plants,' I told him. 'Can't be.'

The sound mounted in intensity, scraping the edges off my occipital bones. I was about to go down to the shop when Harry and Tony leapt out of their chairs and dived back against the wall.

'Steve, look out!' Tony yelled at me. He pointed wildly at the table I was leaning on, picked up a chair and smashed it down on the glass top.

I stood up and brushed the fragments out of my hair.

'What the hell's the matter?'

Tony was looking down at the tangle of wickerwork tied round the metal struts of the table. Harry came forward and took my arm gingerly.

'That was close. You all right?'

'It's gone,' Tony said flatly. He looked carefully over the balcony floor and down over the rail into the street.

'What was it?' I asked.

Harry peered at me closely. 'Didn't you see it? It was about three inches from you. Emperor scorpion, big as a lobster.' He sat down weakly on a beer crate. 'Must have been a sonic one. The noise has gone now.'

After they'd left I cleared up the mess and had a quiet beer to myself. I could have sworn nothing had got on to the table.

On the balcony opposite, wearing a gown of ionized fibre, the golden woman was watching me.

I found out who she was the next morning. Tony and Harry were down at the beach with their wives, probably enlarging on the scorpion, and I was in the shop tuning up a Khan-Arachnid orchid with the UV lamp. It was a difficult bloom, with a normal full range of twenty-four octaves, but unless it got a lot of exercise it tended to relapse into neurotic minor-key transpositions which were the devil to break. And as the senior bloom in the shop it naturally affected all the others. Invariably when I opened the shop in the mornings, it sounded like a madhouse, but as soon as I'd fed the Arachnid and straightened out one or two pH gradients the rest promptly took their cues from it and dimmed down quietly in their control tanks, two-time, three-four, the multi-tones, all in perfect harmony.

There were only about a dozen true Arachnids in captivity; most of the others were either mutes or grafts from dicot stems, and I was lucky to have mine at all. I'd bought the place five years earlier from an old half-deaf man called Sayers, and the day before he left he moved a lot of rogue stock out to the garbage disposal scoop behind the apartment block. Reclaiming some of the tanks, I'd come across the Arachnid, thriving on a diet of algae and perished rubber tubing.

Why Sayers had wanted to throw it away I had never discovered. Before he came to Vermilion Sands he'd been a curator at the Kew Conservatoire where the first choro-flora had been bred, and had worked under the Director, Dr Mandel. As a young botanist of twenty-five Mandel had discovered the prime Arachnid in the Guiana forest. The orchid took its name from the Khan-Arachnid spider which pollinated the flower, simultaneously laying its own eggs in the fleshy ovule, guided, or as Mandel always insisted, actually mesmerized to it by the vibrations which the orchid's calyx emitted at pollination time. The first Arachnid orchids beamed out only a few random frequencies, but by cross-breeding and maintaining them artificially at the pollination stage Mandel had produced a strain that spanned a maximum of twenty-four octaves.

Not that he had ever been able to hear them. At the climax of his life's work Mandel, like Beethoven, was stone deaf, but apparently by merely looking at a blossom he could listen to its music. Strangely though, after he went deaf he never looked at an Arachnid.

That morning I could almost understand why. The orchid was in a vicious mood. First it refused to feed, and I had to coax it along in a fluoraldehyde flush, and then it started going ultra-sonic, which meant complaints from all the dog owners in the area. Finally it tried to fracture the tank by resonating.

The whole place was in uproar, and I was almost resigned to shutting them down and waking them all by hand individually – a backbreaking job with eighty tanks in the shop – when everything suddenly died away to a murmur.

I looked round and saw the golden-skinned woman walk in.

'Good morning,' I said. 'They must like you.'

She laughed pleasantly. 'Hello. Weren't they behaving?'

Under the black beach robe her skin was a softer, more mellow gold, and it was her eyes that held me. I could just see them under the wide-brimmed hat. Insect legs wavered delicately round two points of purple light.

She walked over to a bank of mixed ferns and stood looking at them. The ferns reached out towards her and trebled eagerly in their liquid fluted voices.

'Aren't they sweet?' she said, stroking the fronds gently. 'They need so much affection.'

Her voice was low in the register, a breath of cool sand pouring, with a lilt that gave it music.

'I've just come to Vermilion Sands,' she said, 'and my apartment seems awfully quiet. Perhaps if I had a flower, one would be enough, I shouldn't feel so lonely.'

I couldn't take my eyes off her.

'Yes,' I agreed, brisk and businesslike. 'What about something colourful? This Sumatra Samphire, say? It's a pedigree mezzo-soprano from the same follicle as the Bayreuth Festival Prima Belladonna.'

'No,' she said. 'It looks rather cruel.'

'Or this Louisiana Lute Lily? If you thin out its SO_2 it'll play some beautiful madrigals. I'll show you how to do it.'

She wasn't listening to me. Slowly, her hands raised in front of her breasts so that she almost seemed to be praying, she moved towards the display counter on which the Arachnid stood.

'How beautiful it is,' she said, gazing at the rich yellow and purple leaves hanging from the scarlet-ribbed vibrocalyx.

I followed her across the floor and switched on the Arachnid's audio so that she could hear it. Immediately the plant came to life. The leaves stiffened and filled with colour and the calyx inflated, its ribs sprung tautly. A few sharp disconnected notes spat out.

'Beautiful, but evil,' I said.

'Evil?' she repeated. 'No, proud.' She stepped closer to the orchid and looked down into its malevolent head. The Arachnid quivered and the spines on its stem arched and flexed menacingly.

'Careful,' I warned her. 'It's sensitive to the faintest respiratory sounds.'

'Quiet,' she said, waving me back. 'I think it wants to sing.'

'Those are only key fragments,' I told her. 'It doesn't perform. I use it as a frequency –'

'Listen!' She held my arm and squeezed it tightly.

A low, rhythmic fusion of melody had been coming from the plants around the shop, and mounting above them I heard a single stronger voice calling out, at first a thin high-pitched reed of sound that began to pulse and deepen and finally swelled into full baritone, raising the other plants in chorus about itself.

I had never heard the Arachnid sing before. I was listening to it open-eared when I felt a glow of heat burn against my arm. I turned and saw the woman staring intently at the plant, her skin aflame, the insects in her eyes writhing insanely. The Arachnid stretched out towards her, calyx erect, leaves like blood-red sabres.

I stepped round her quickly and switched off the argon feed. The Arachnid sank to a whimper, and around us there was a nightmarish babel of broken notes and voices toppling from high C's and L's into discord. A faint whispering of leaves moved over the silence.

The woman gripped the edge of the tank and gathered herself. Her skin dimmed and the insects in her eyes slowed to a delicate wavering.

'Why did you turn it off?' she asked heavily.

'I'm sorry,' I said. 'But I've got ten thousand dollars' worth of stock here and that sort of twelve-tone emotional storm can blow a lot of valves. Most of these plants aren't equipped for grand opera.'

She watched the Arachnid as the gas drained out of its calyx. One by one its leaves buckled and lost their colour.

'How much is it?' she asked me, opening her bag.

'It's not for sale,' I said. 'Frankly I've no idea how it picked up those bars –'

'Will a thousand dollars be enough?' she asked, her eyes fixed on me steadily.

'I can't,' I told her. 'I'd never be able to tune the others without it. Anyway,' I added, trying to smile, 'that Arachnid would be dead in ten minutes if you took it out of its vivarium. All these cylinders and leads would look a little odd inside your lounge.'

'Yes, of course,' she agreed, suddenly smiling back at me. 'I was stupid.' She gave the orchid a last backward glance and strolled away across the floor to the long Tchaikovsky section popular with the tourists.

'Pathétique,' she read off a label at random. 'I'll take this.'

I wrapped up the scabia and slipped the instructional booklet into the crate, keeping my eye on her all the time.

'Don't look so alarmed,' she said with amusement. 'I've never heard anything like that before.'

I wasn't alarmed. It was that thirty years at Vermilion Sands had narrowed my horizons.

'How long are you staying at Vermilion Sands?' I asked her.

'I open at the Casino tonight,' she said. She told me her name was Jane Ciracylides and that she was a speciality singer.

'Why don't you look in?' she asked, her eyes fluttering mischievously. 'I come on at eleven. You may find it interesting.'

I did. The next morning Vermilion Sands hummed. Jane created a

sensation. After her performance three hundred people swore they'd
seen everything from a choir of angels taking the vocal in the music
of the spheres to Alexander's Ragtime Band. As for myself, perhaps I'd
listened to too many flowers, but at least I knew where the scorpion on
the balcony had come from.

Tony Miles had heard Sophie Tucker singing the 'St Louis Blues', and
Harry, the elder Bach conducting the B Minor Mass.

They came round to the shop and argued over their respective perfor-
mances while I wrestled with the flowers.

'Amazing,' Tony exclaimed. 'How does she do it? Tell me.'

'The Heidelberg score,' Harry ecstased. 'Sublime, absolute.' He looked
irritably at the flowers. 'Can't you keep these things quiet? They're making
one hell of a row.'

They were, and I had a shrewd idea why. The Arachnid was completely
out of control, and by the time I'd clamped it down in a weak saline it
had blown out over three hundred dollars' worth of shrubs.

'The performance at the Casino last night was nothing on the one she
gave here yesterday,' I told them. '*The Ring of the Niebelungs* played by
Stan Kenton. That Arachnid went insane. I'm sure it wanted to kill her.'

Harry watched the plant convulsing its leaves in rigid spasmic move-
ments.

'If you ask me it's in an advanced state of rut. Why should it want to
kill her?'

'Her voice must have overtones that irritate its calyx. None of the other
plants minded. They cooed like turtle doves when she touched them.'

Tony shivered happily.

Light dazzled in the street outside.

I handed Tony the broom. 'Here, lover, brace yourself on that. Miss
Ciracylides is dying to meet you.'

Jane came into the shop, wearing a flame yellow cocktail skirt and
another of her hats.

I introduced her to Harry and Tony.

'The flowers seem very quiet this morning,' she said. 'What's the matter
with them?'

'I'm cleaning out the tanks,' I told her. 'By the way, we all want to
congratulate you on last night. How does it feel to be able to name your
fiftieth city?'

She smiled shyly and sauntered away round the shop. As I knew she
would, she stopped by the Arachnid and levelled her eyes at it.

I wanted to see what she'd say, but Harry and Tony were all around
her, and soon got her up to my apartment, where they had a hilarious
morning playing the fool and raiding my scotch.

'What about coming out with us after the show tonight?' Tony asked
her. 'We can go dancing at the Flamingo.'

'But you're both married,' Jane protested. 'Aren't you worried about
your reputations?'

'Oh, we'll bring the girls,' Harry said airily. 'And Steve here can come along and hold your coat.'

We played i-Go together. Jane said she'd never played the game before, but she had no difficulty picking up the rules, and when she started sweeping the board with us I knew she was cheating. Admittedly it isn't every day that you get a chance to play i-Go with a golden-skinned woman with insects for eyes, but never the less I was annoyed. Harry and Tony, of course, didn't mind.

'She's charming,' Harry said, after she'd left. 'Who cares? It's a stupid game anyway.'

'I care,' I said. 'She cheats.'

The next three or four days at the shop were an audio-vegetative armageddon. Jane came in every morning to look at the Arachnid, and her presence was more than the flower could bear. Unfortunately I couldn't starve the plants below their thresholds. They needed exercise and they had to have the Arachnid to lead them. But instead of running through its harmonic scales the orchid only screeched and whined. It wasn't the noise, which only a couple of dozen people complained about, but the damage being done to their vibratory chords that worried me. Those in the seventeenth century catalogues stood up well to the strain, and the moderns were immune, but the Romantics burst their calyxes by the score. By the third day after Jane's arrival I'd lost two hundred dollars' worth of Beethoven and more Mendelssohn and Schubert than I could bear to think about.

Jane seemed oblivious to the trouble she was causing me.

'What's wrong with them all?' she asked, surveying the chaos of gas cylinders and drip feeds spread across the floor.

'I don't think they like you,' I told her. 'At least the Arachnid doesn't. Your voice may move men to strange and wonderful visions, but it throws that orchid into acute melancholia.'

'Nonsense,' she said, laughing at me. 'Give it to me and I'll show you how to look after it.'

'Are Tony and Harry keeping you happy?' I asked her. I was annoyed that I couldn't go down to the beach with them and instead had to spend my time draining tanks and titrating up norm solutions, none of which ever worked.

'They're very amusing,' she said. 'We play i-Go and I sing for them. But I wish you could come out more often.'

After another two weeks I had to give up. I decided to close the plants down until Jane had left Vermilion Sands. I knew it would take me three months to rescore the stock, but I had no alternative.

The next day I received a large order for mixed coloratura herbaceous from the Santiago Garden Choir. They wanted delivery in three weeks.

'I'm sorry,' Jane said, when she heard I wouldn't be able to fill the order. 'You must wish that I'd never come to Vermilion Sands.'

She stared thoughtfully into one of the darkened tanks.

'Couldn't I score them for you?' she suggested.

'No thanks,' I said, laughing. 'I've had enough of that already.'

'Don't be silly, of course I could.'

I shook my head.

Tony and Harry told me I was crazy.

'Her voice has a wide enough range,' Tony said. 'You admit it your-self.'

'What have you got against her?' Harry asked. 'That she cheats at i-Go?'

'It's nothing to do with that,' I said. 'And her voice has a wider range than you think.'

We played i-Go at Jane's apartment. Jane won ten dollars from each of us.

'I am lucky,' she said, very pleased with herself. 'I never seem to lose.' She counted up the bills and put them away carefully in her bag, her golden skin glowing.

Then Santiago sent me a repeat query.

I found Jane down among the cafés, holding off a siege of admirers.

'Have you given in yet?' she asked me, smiling at the young men.

'I don't know what you're doing to me,' I said, 'but anything is worth trying.'

Back at the shop I raised a bank of perennials past their thresholds. Jane helped me attach the gas and fluid lines.

'We'll try these first,' I said. 'Frequencies 543–785. Here's the score.'

Jane took off her hat and began to ascend the scale, her voice clear and pure. At first the Columbine hesitated and Jane went down again and drew them along with her. They went up a couple of octaves together and then the plants stumbled and went off at a tangent of stepped chords.

'Try K sharp,' I said. I fed a little chlorous acid into the tank and the Columbine followed her up eagerly, the infra-calyxes warbling delicate variations on the treble clef.

'Perfect,' I said.

It took us only four hours to fill the order.

'You're better than the Arachnid,' I congratulated her. 'How would you like a job? I'll fit you out with a large cool tank and all the chlorine you can breathe.'

'Careful,' she told me. 'I may say yes. Why don't we rescore a few more of them while we're about it?'

'You're tired,' I said. 'Let's go and have a drink.'

'Let me try the Arachnid,' she suggested. 'That would be more of a challenge.'

Her eyes never left the flower. I wondered what they'd do if I left them together. Try to sing each other to death?

'No,' I said. 'Tomorrow perhaps.'

We sat on the balcony together, glasses at our elbows, and talked the afternoon away.

She told me little about herself, but I gathered that her father had been a mining engineer in Peru and her mother a dancer at a Lima vu-tavern. They'd wandered from deposit to deposit, the father digging his concessions, the mother signing on at the nearest bordello to pay the rent.

'She only sang, of course,' Jane added. 'Until my father came.' She blew bubbles into her glass. 'So you think I give them what they want at the Casino. By the way, what do you see?'

'I'm afraid I'm your one failure,' I said. 'Nothing. Except you.'

She dropped her eyes. 'That sometimes happens,' she said. 'I'm glad this time.'

A million suns pounded inside me. Until then I'd been reserving judgment on myself.

Harry and Tony were polite, if disappointed.

'I can't believe it,' Harry said sadly. 'I won't. How did you do it?'

'That mystical left-handed approach, of course,' I told him. 'All ancient seas and dark wells.'

'What's she like?' Tony asked eagerly. 'I mean, does she burn or just tingle?'

Jane sang at the Casino every night from eleven to three, but apart from that I suppose we were always together. Sometimes in the late afternoons we'd drive out along the beach to the Scented Desert and sit alone by one of the pools, watching the sun fall away behind the reefs and hills, lulling ourselves on the rose-sick air. When the wind began to blow cool across the sand we'd slip down into the water, bathe ourselves and drive back to town, filling the streets and café terraces with jasmine and musk-rose and helianthemum.

On other evenings we'd go down to one of the quiet bars at Lagoon West, and have supper out on the flats, and Jane would tease the waiters and sing honeybirds and angelcakes to the children who came in across the sand to watch her.

I realize now that I must have achieved a certain notoriety along the beach, but I didn't mind giving the old women – and beside Jane they all seemed to be old women – something to talk about. During the Recess no one cared very much about anything, and for that reason I never questioned myself too closely over my affair with Jane Ciracylides. As I sat on the balcony with her looking out over the cool early evenings or felt her body glowing beside me in the darkness I allowed myself few anxieties.

Absurdly, the only disagreement I ever had with her was over her cheating.

I remember that I once taxed her with it.

'Do you know you've taken over five hundred dollars from me, Jane? You're still doing it. Even now!'

She laughed impishly. 'Do I cheat? I'll let you win one day.'

'But why do you?' I insisted.

'It's more fun to cheat,' she said. 'Otherwise it's so boring.'

'Where will you go when you leave Vermilion Sands?' I asked her.

She looked at me in surprise. 'Why do you say that? I don't think I shall ever leave.'

'Don't tease me, Jane. You're a child of another world than this.'

'My father came from Peru,' she reminded me.

'But you didn't get your voice from him,' I said. 'I wish I could have heard your mother sing. Had she a better voice than yours, Jane?'

'She thought so. My father couldn't stand either of us.'

That was the evening I last saw Jane. We'd changed, and in the half an hour before she left for the Casino we sat on the balcony and I listened to her voice, like a spectral fountain, pour its luminous notes into the air. The music remained with me even after she'd gone, hanging faintly in the darkness around her chair.

I felt curiously sleepy, almost sick on the air she'd left behind, and at 11.30, when I knew she'd be appearing on stage at the Casino, I went out for a walk along the beach.

As I left the elevator I heard music coming from the shop.

At first I thought I'd left one of the audio switches on, but I knew the voice only too well.

The windows of the shop had been shuttered, so I got in through the passage which led from the garage courtyard round at the back of the apartment house.

The lights had been turned out, but a brilliant glow filled the shop, throwing a golden fire on to the tanks along the counters. Across the ceiling liquid colours danced in reflection.

The music I had heard before, but only in overture.

The Arachnid had grown to three times its size. It towered nine feet high out of the shattered lid of the control tank, leaves tumid and inflamed, its calyx as large as a bucket, raging insanely.

Arched forwards into it, her head thrown back, was Jane.

I ran over to her, my eyes filling with light, and grabbed her arm, trying to pull her away from it.

'Jane!' I shouted over the noise. 'Get down!'

She flung my hand away. In her eyes, fleetingly, was a look of shame.

While I was sitting on the stairs in the entrance Tony and Harry drove up.

'Where's Jane?' Harry asked. 'Has anything happened to her? We were down at the Casino.' They both turned towards the music. 'What the hell's going on?'

Tony peered at me suspiciously. 'Steve, anything wrong?'

Harry dropped the bouquet he was carrying and started towards the rear entrance.

'Harry!' I shouted after him. 'Get back!'

Tony held my shoulder. 'Is Jane in there?'

I caught them as they opened the door into the shop.

'Good God!' Harry yelled. 'Let go of me, you fool!' He struggled to get away from me. 'Steve, it's trying to kill her!'

I jammed the door shut and held them back.

I never saw Jane again. The three of us waited in my apartment. When the music died away we went down and found the shop in darkness. The Arachnid had shrunk to its normal size.

The next day it died.

Where Jane went to I don't know. Not long afterwards the Recess ended, and the big government schemes came along and started up all the clocks and kept us too busy working off the lost time to worry about a few bruised petals. Harry told me that Jane had been seen on her way through Red Beach, and I heard recently that someone very like her was doing the nightclubs this side out of Pernambuco.

So if any of you around here keep a choro-florist's, and have a Khan-Arachnid orchid, look out for a golden-skinned woman with insects for eyes. Perhaps she'll play i-Go with you, and I'm sorry to have to say it, but she'll always cheat.

1956

ESCAPEMENT

Neither of us was watching the play too closely when I first noticed the slip. I was stretched back in front of the fire with the crossword, braising gently and toying with 17 down ('told by antique clocks? 5, 5.') while Helen was hemming an old petticoat, looking up only when the third lead, a heavy-chinned youth with a 42-inch neck and a base-surge voice, heaved manfully downscreen. The play was 'My Sons, My Sons', one of those Thursday night melodramas Channel 2 put out through the winter months, and had been running for about an hour; we'd reached that ebb somewhere round Act 3 Scene 3 just after the old farmer learns that his sons no longer respect him. The whole play must have been recorded on film, and it sounded extremely funny to switch from the old man's broken mutterings back to the showdown sequence fifteen minutes earlier when the eldest son starts drumming his chest and dragging in the high symbols. Somewhere an engineer was out of a job.

'They've got their reels crossed,' I told Helen. 'This is where we came in.'

'Is it?' she said, looking up. 'I wasn't watching. Tap the set.'

'Just wait and see. In a moment everyone in the studio will start apologizing.'

Helen peered at the screen. 'I don't think we've seen this,' she said. 'I'm sure we haven't. Quiet.'

I shrugged and went back to 17 down, thinking vaguely about sand dials and water clocks. The scene dragged on; the old man stood his ground, ranted over his turnips and thundered desperately for Ma. The studio must have decided to run it straight through again and pretend no one had noticed. Even so they'd be fifteen minutes behind their schedule.

Ten minutes later it happened again.

I sat up. 'That's funny,' I said slowly. 'Haven't they spotted it yet? They can't all be asleep.'

'What's the matter?' Helen asked, looking up from her needle basket. 'Is something wrong with the set?'

'I thought you were watching. I told you we'd seen this before. Now they're playing it back for the third time.'

'They're not,' Helen insisted. 'I'm sure they aren't. You must have read the book.'

'Heaven forbid.' I watched the set closely. Any minute now an announcer spitting on a sandwich would splutter red-faced to the screen. I'm not

12

one of those people who reach for their phones every time someone mispronounces meteorology, but this time I knew there'd be thousands who'd feel it their duty to keep the studio exchanges blocked all night. And for any go-ahead comedian on a rival station the lapse was a god-send.

'Do you mind if I change the programme?' I asked Helen. 'See if anything else is on.'

'Don't. This is the most interesting part of the play. You'll spoil it.'

'Darling, you're not even watching. I'll come back to it in a moment, I promise.'

On Channel 5 a panel of three professors and a chorus girl were staring hard at a Roman pot. The question-master, a suave-voiced Oxford don, kept up a lot of crazy patter about scraping the bottom of the barrow. The professors seemed stumped, but the girl looked as if she knew exactly what went into the pot but didn't dare say it.

On 9 there was a lot of studio laughter and someone was giving a sports-car to an enormous woman in a cartwheel hat. The woman nervously ducked her head away from the camera and stared glumly at the car. The compère opened the door for her and I was wondering whether she'd try to get into it when Helen cut in:

'Harry, don't be mean. You're just playing.'

I turned back to the play on Channel 2. The same scene was on, nearing the end of its run.

'Now watch it,' I told Helen. She usually managed to catch on the third time round. 'Put that sewing away, it's getting on my nerves. God, I know this off by heart.'

'Sh!' Helen told me. 'Can't you stop talking?'

I lit a cigarette and lay back in the sofa, waiting. The apologies, to say the least, would have to be magniloquent. Two ghost runs at £100 a minute totted up to a tidy heap of doubloons.

The scene drew to a close, the old man stared heavily at his boots, the dusk drew down and –

We were back where we started from.

'Fantastic!' I said, standing up and turning some snow off the screen. 'It's incredible.'

'I didn't know you enjoyed this sort of play,' Helen said calmly. 'You never used to.' She glanced over at the screen and then went back to her petticoat.

I watched her warily. A million years earlier I'd probably have run howling out of the cave and flung myself thankfully under the nearest dinosaur. Nothing in the meanwhile had lessened the dangers hemming in the undaunted husband.

'Darling,' I explained patiently, just keeping the edge out of my voice, 'in case you hadn't noticed they are now playing this same scene through for the fourth time.'

'The fourth time?' Helen said doubtfully. 'Are they repeating it?'

*   *   *

I was visualizing a studio full of announcers and engineers slumped unconscious over their mikes and valves, while an automatic camera pumped out the same reel. Eerie but unlikely. There were monitor receivers as well as the critics, agents, sponsors, and, unforgivably, the playwright himself weighing every minute and every word in their private currencies. They'd all have a lot to say under tomorrow's headlines.

'Sit down and stop fidgeting,' Helen said. 'Have you lost your bone?'

I felt round the cushions and ran my hand along the carpet below the sofa.

'My cigarette,' I said. 'I must have thrown it into the fire. I don't think I dropped it.'

I turned back to the set and switched on the give-away programme, noting the time, 9.03, so that I could get back to Channel 2 at 9.15. When the explanation came I just had to hear it.

'I thought you were enjoying the play,' Helen said. 'Why've you turned it off?'

I gave her what sometimes passes in our flat for a withering frown and settled back.

The enormous woman was still at it in front of the cameras, working her way up a pyramid of questions on cookery. The audience was subdued but interest mounted. Eventually she answered the jack-pot question and the audience roared and thumped their seats like a lot of madmen. The compère led her across the stage to another sports car.

'She'll have a stable of them soon,' I said aside to Helen.

The woman shook hands and awkwardly dipped the brim of her hat, smiling nervously with embarrassment.

The gesture was oddly familiar.

I jumped up and switched to Channel 5. The panel were still staring hard at their pot.

Then I started to realize what was going on.

All three programmes were repeating themselves.

'Helen,' I said over my shoulder. 'Get me a scotch and soda, will you?'

'What *is* the matter? Have you strained your back?'

'Quickly, quickly!' I snapped my fingers.

'Hold on.' She got up and went into the pantry.

I looked at the time. 9.12. Then I returned to the play and kept my eyes glued to the screen. Helen came back and put something down on the end-table.

'There you are. You all right?'

When it switched I thought I was ready for it, but the surprise must have knocked me flat. I found myself lying out on the sofa. The first thing I did was reach round for the drink.

'Where did you put it?' I asked Helen.

'What?'

'The scotch. You brought it in a couple of minutes ago. It was on the table.'

'You've been dreaming,' she said gently. She leant forward and started watching the play.

I went into the pantry and found the bottle. As I filled a tumbler I noticed the clock over the kitchen sink. 9.07. An hour slow, now that I thought about it. But my wristwatch said 9.05, and always ran perfectly. And the clock on the mantelpiece in the lounge also said 9.05.

Before I really started worrying I had to make sure.

Mullvaney, our neighbour in the flat above, opened his door when I knocked.

'Hello, Bartley. Corkscrew?'

'No, no,' I told him. 'What's the right time? Our clocks are going crazy.'

He glanced at his wrist. 'Nearly ten past.'

'Nine or ten?'

He looked at his watch again. 'Nine, should be. What's up?'

'I don't know whether I'm losing my –' I started to say. Then I stopped.

Mullvaney eyed me curiously. Over his shoulder I heard a wave of studio applause, broken by the creamy, unctuous voice of the giveaway compère.

'How long's that programme been on?' I asked him.

'About twenty minutes. Aren't you watching?'

'No,' I said, adding casually, 'Is anything wrong with your set?'

He shook his head. 'Nothing. Why?'

'Mine's chasing its tail. Anyway, thanks.'

'OK,' he said. He watched me go down the stairs and shrugged as he shut his door.

I went into the hall, picked up the phone and dialled.

'Hello, Tom?' Tom Farnold works the desk next to mine at the office. 'Tom, Harry here. What time do you make it?'

'Time the liberals were back.'

'No, seriously.'

'Let's see. Twelve past nine. By the way, did you find those pickles I left for you in the safe?'

'Yeah, thanks. Listen, Tom,' I went on, 'the goddamdest things are happening here. We were watching Diller's play on Channel 2 when –'

'I'm watching it now. Hurry it up.'

'You are? Well, how do you explain this repetition business? And the way the clocks are stuck between 9 and 9.15?'

Tom laughed. 'I don't know,' he said. 'I suggest you go outside and give the house a shake.'

I reached out for the glass I had with me on the hall table, wondering how to explain to –

The next moment I found myself back on the sofa. I was holding the newspaper and looking at 17 down. A part of my mind was thinking about antique clocks.

I pulled myself out of it and glanced across at Helen. She was sitting quietly with her needle basket. The all too familiar play was repeating itself and by the clock on the mantelpiece it was still just after 9.

I went back into the hall and dialled Tom again, trying not to stampede myself. In some way, I hadn't begun to understand how, a section of time was spinning round in a circle, with myself in the centre.

'Tom,' I asked quickly as soon as he picked up the phone. 'Did I call you five minutes ago?'

'Who's that again?'

'Harry here. Harry Bartley. Sorry, Tom.' I paused and rephrased the question, trying to make it sound intelligible. 'Tom, did you phone me up about five minutes ago? We've had a little trouble with the line here.'

'No,' he told me. 'Wasn't me. By the way, did you get those pickles I left in the safe?'

'Thanks a lot,' I said, beginning to panic. 'Are you watching the play, Tom?'

'Yes. I think I'll get back to it. See you.'

I went into the kitchen and had a long close look at myself in the mirror. A crack across it dropped one side of my face three inches below the other, but apart from that I couldn't see anything that added up to a psychosis. My eyes seemed steady, pulse was in the low seventies, no tics or clammy traumatic sweat. Everything around me seemed much too solid and authentic for a dream.

I waited for a minute and then went back to the lounge and sat down. Helen was watching the play.

I leant forward and turned the knob round. The picture dimmed and swayed off.

'Harry, I'm watching that! Don't switch it off.'

I went over to her. 'Poppet,' I said, holding my voice together. 'Listen to me, please. Very carefully. It's important.'

She frowned, put her sewing down and took my hands.

'For some reason, I don't know why, we seem to be in a sort of circular time trap, just going round and round. You're not aware of it, and I can't find anyone else who is either.'

Helen stared at me in amazement. 'Harry,' she started, 'what are you –'

'Helen!' I insisted, gripping her shoulders. 'Listen! For the last two hours a section of time about 15 minutes long has been repeating itself. The clocks are stuck between 9 and 9.15. That play you're watching has –'

'Harry, darling.' She looked at me and smiled helplessly. 'You are silly. Now turn it on again.'

I gave up.

*   *   *

As I switched the set on I ran through all the other channels just to see if anything had changed.

The panel stared at their pot, the fat woman won her sports car, the old farmer ranted. On Channel 1, the old BBC service which put out a couple of hours on alternate evenings, two newspaper men were interviewing a scientific pundit who appeared on popular educational programmes.

'What effect these dense eruptions of gas will have so far it's impossible to tell. However, there's certainly no cause for any alarm. These billows have mass, and I think we can expect a lot of strange optical effects as the light leaving the sun is deflected by them gravitationally.'

He started playing with a set of coloured celluloid balls running on concentric metal rings, and fiddled with a ripple tank mounted against a mirror on the table.

One of the newsmen asked: 'What about the relationship between light and time? If I remember my relativity they're tied up together pretty closely. Are you sure we won't all need to add another hand to our clocks and watches?'

The pundit smiled. 'I think we'll be able to get along without that. Time is extremely complicated, but I can assure you the clocks won't suddenly start running backwards or sideways.'

I listened to him until Helen began to remonstrate. I switched the play on for her and went off into the hall. The fool didn't know what he was talking about. What I couldn't understand was why I was the only person who realized what was going on. If I could get Tom over I might just be able to convince him.

I picked up the phone and glanced at my watch.

9.13. By the time I got through to Tom the next changeover would be due. Somehow I didn't like the idea of being picked up and flung to the sofa, however painless it might be. I put the phone down and went into the lounge.

The jump-back was smoother than I expected. I wasn't conscious of anything, not even the slightest tremor. A phrase was stuck in my mind: Olden Times.

The newspaper was back on my lap, folded around the crossword. I looked through the clues.

17 down: Told by antique clocks? 5, 5.

I must have solved it subconsciously.

I remembered that I'd intended to phone Tom.

'Hullo, Tom?' I asked when I got through. 'Harry here.'

'Did you get those pickles I left in the safe?'

'Yes, thanks a lot. Tom, could you come round tonight? Sorry to ask you this late, but it's fairly urgent.'

'Yes, of course,' he said. 'What's the trouble?'

'I'll tell you when you get here. As soon as you can?'

'Sure. I'll leave right away. Is Helen all right?'

'Yes, she's fine. Thanks again.'

I went into the dining room and pulled a bottle of gin and a couple of tonics out of the sideboard. He'd need a drink when he heard what I had to say.

Then I realized he'd never make it. From Earls Court it would take him at least half an hour to reach us at Maida Vale and he'd probably get no further than Marble Arch.

I filled my glass out of the virtually bottomless bottle of scotch and tried to work out a plan of action.

The first step was to get hold of someone like myself who retained his awareness of the past switch-backs. Somewhere else there must be others trapped in their little 15-minute cages who were also wondering desperately how to get out. I could start by phoning everyone I knew and then going on at random through the phonebook. But what could we do if we did find each other? In fact there was nothing to do except sit tight and wait for it all to wear off. At least I knew I wasn't looping my loop. Once these billows or whatever they were had burnt themselves out we'd be able to get off the round-about.

Until then I had an unlimited supply of whisky waiting for me in the half-empty bottle standing on the sink, though of course there was one snag: I'd never be able to get drunk.

I was musing round some of the other possibilities available and wondering how to get a permanent record of what was going on when an idea hit me.

I got out the phone-directory and looked up the number of KBC-TV, Channel 9.

A girl at reception answered the phone. After haggling with her for a couple of minutes I persuaded her to put me through to one of the producers.

'Hullo,' I said. 'Is the jackpot question in tonight's programme known to any members of the studio audience?'

'No, of course not.'

'I see. As a matter of interest, do you yourself know it?'

'No,' he said. 'All the questions tonight are known only to our senior programme producer and M. Phillipe Soisson of Savoy Hotels Limited. They're a closely guarded secret.'

'Thanks,' I said. 'If you've got a piece of paper handy I'll give you the jackpot question. "List the complete menu at the Guildhall Coronation Banquet in July 1953."'

There were muttered consultations, and a second voice came through.

'Who's that speaking?'

'Mr H.R. Bartley, 129b Sutton Court Road, N.W. –'

Before I could finish I found myself back in the lounge.

The jump-back had caught me. But instead of being stretched out on the sofa I was standing up, leaning on one elbow against the mantelpiece, looking down at the newspaper.